18

This book belongs to:

Digital art by Callaway Animation Studios under the direction of David Kirk
in collaboration with Nelvana Limited.

This book is based on the TV episode "A Cloudy Day in Sunny Patch," written by Steven Sullivan,
from the animated TV series *Miss Spider's Sunny Patch Friends* on Nick Jr.,
a Nelvana Limited/Absolute Pictures Limited co-production in association
with Callaway Arts & Entertainment, based on the Miss Spider books by David Kirk.

Nicholas Callaway, President and Publisher
Cathy Ferrara, Managing Editor and Production Director
Antoinette White, Senior Editor • Toshiya Masuda, Art Director
George Gould, Director of Digital Services • Joya Rajadhyaksha, Associate Editor
Doug Vitarelli, Director of Animation • Raphael Shea, Art Assistant • Cara Paul, Digital Artist
Amy Cloud, Assistant Editor • Krupa Jhaveri, Design Assistant • Alex Ballas, Design Assistant

Special thanks to the Nelvana staff, including Doug Murphy, Scott Dyer, Tracy Ewing, Pam Lehn,
Tonya Lindo, Mark Picard, Susie Grondin, Luis Lopez, Eric Pentz, and Georgina Robinson.

Library of Congress Cataloging-in-Publication Data available upon request.

Distributed in the United States by Viking Children's Books.

Callaway Arts & Entertainment, its Callaway logotype,
and Callaway & Kirk Company LLC are trademarks.

ISBN 0-448-43897-6

Visit Callaway Arts & Entertainment at www.callaway.com

10 9 8 7 6 5 4 3 2 1 05 06 07 08 09 10

First edition, July 2005

Printed in China

Miss Spider's
A Cloudy Day in Sunny Patch

David Kirk

CALLAWAY

NEW YORK

2005

It was almost Shimmer's eighth hatchday, and she was so excited—her family was throwing her first hatchday party ever!

"Tell me, Shimmer, what kind of party do you want?" asked Miss Spider.

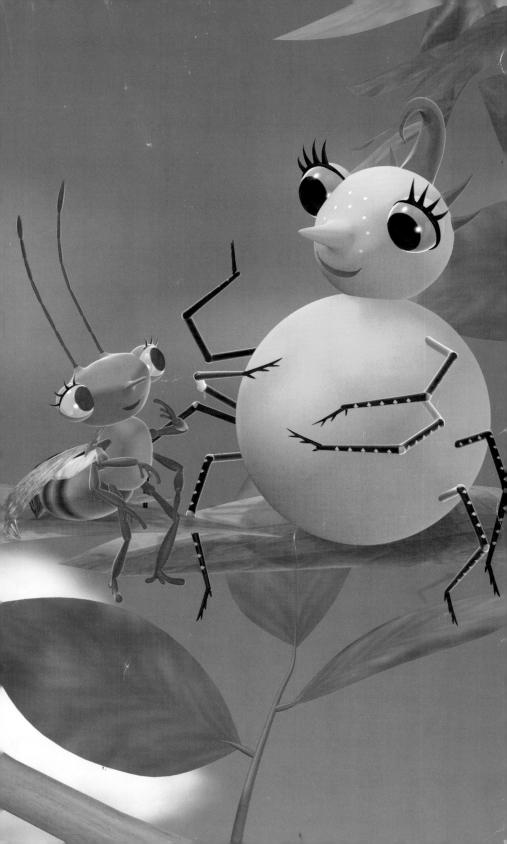

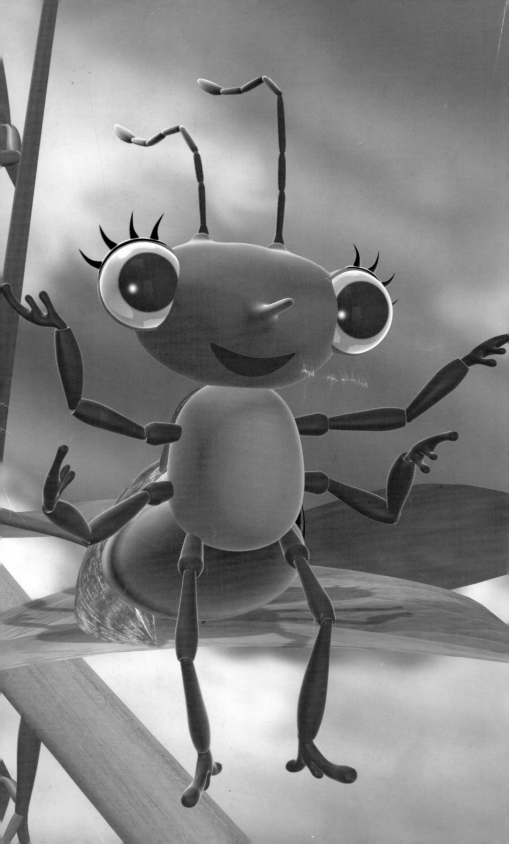

"That's easy!" laughed Shimmer. "I want to have my party at the Taddy Puddle. I want ribbons and flowers and funny hats. I want a great big fruitcake with strawberry lice cream. Then I want to go swimming and play beach buggy-ball!"

Miss Spider and her children planned the party.

"Dragon, Pansy, and I can set up the games!" Squirt said.

"We'll make a web banner with a big number eight!" Snowdrop and Wiggle exclaimed.

"I'll help bake the cake!" said Bounce.

Finally, it was Shimmer's hatchday. Everybuggy was busy getting ready when a rain cloud filled the sky.

Miss Spider looked up and sighed, "Oh no."

Shimmer heard thunder in the distance.

"Is that what I think it is?" she asked.

Rain poured down.
The little bugs ran inside.

Shimmer was miserable.

"I'm sorry, honey," said Miss Spider. "Sometimes nature makes us change our plans."

"We can still have fun," said Squirt. "Let's play hide and seek!"

"I'm it! I'm it! I'm it!" shouted Bounce, closing his eyes and turning his back. "I'll count!"

"But there's no place to hide!" Shimmer whined. "This isn't the hatchday party I wanted at all."

"I know a game you'd love to play!" shouted Dragon. "Beach buggy-ball!"

He took a long swing and smacked the ball with all his might . . .

. . . right into the hatchday cake. Shimmer's eyes filled with tears. She cried harder and harder. Her cries turned to sobs. Her sobs turned into a wail.

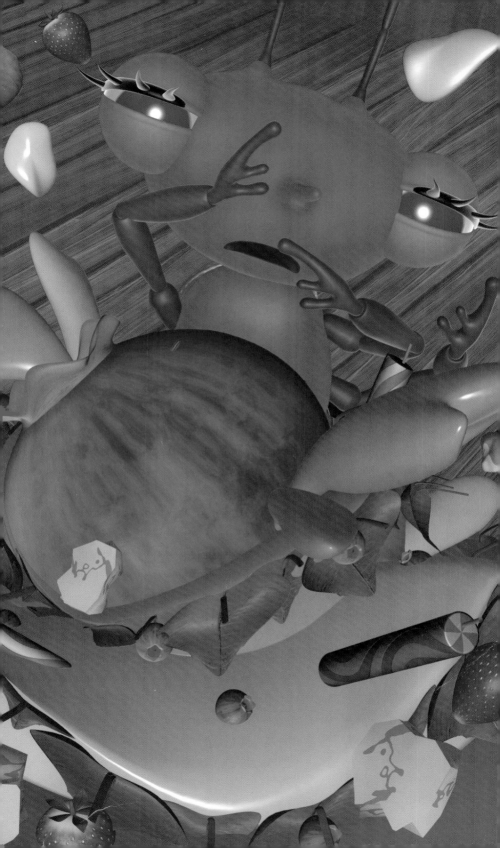

But then her wail turned into a chuckle, her chuckle turned to a giggle, and then finally a great big laugh.

"What's so funny, honey?" asked Miss Spider.

"What's funny?" Shimmer exclaimed. "Just look at us!"

"When your family loves you," Shimmer smiled, "I guess you can have fun doing anything!"